Reverie

Flairs and Glairs

Publication House

"Reverie"

ISBN No: " 978-93-90416-86-8"
1st Edition
Language – English

Flairs and Glairs
Publication House
Regd. Under MSME Act.

Copyright. 2020, Tanishka Dhama

Disclaimer

This is a work of fiction and solely represent the thoughts of the corresponding author of the articles. Our editors have tried their best to edit the content of all the author and check the plagiarism.

All the write-ups in this book are unique and are only published in this book.

In case any plagiarism or error is found, only the author is responsible alone, and not the publisher

Cover Designing and Book Formatting
Shubham Shah

Tanishka Dhama is a 2003-born, Jaipur based poet, author, and blogger. Her interest in poetry emerged at the age of nine when she first started writing. Her interest in classic English Literature, and a passion for Psychology, has helped her comprehend the many layers of human psyche and considers herself an aesthete. Tanishka is also a Tarot Card Reader and is the receiver of many accolades and achievements for her expression in writing as well as speaking.

Her book, Reverie, talks about the various thoughts that cross the human mind at least once in a lifetime and the fantastical world they create, along with the happenings in the real world.

Her

Her nightmare is marked by the sound of the bassoon
Her dreams, wrapped and wrecked soon
She will be shipped like a cargo for sale
In society she passed, in life she failed.

The flowery chains carved on her hands
Tightened around like a bloody band
Her parents agreed her to be a man's tool
She would've been her own mechanic, if they just sent
her to school.

The joys of marriage hid the smirks of money
The sly poison came to her covered in honey
The sound of beating drums felt so wrong
When she craved to hear her school bell dong.

The knowledge she gained, all went to drain
Like tears flowing in the rain
Now she'll be no doctor who wanted to help
What good be a doctor who can't help herself?

And away she goes with that forever stranger
To be educated was to be a danger
She was every girl who had been caught
Forget her name, but forget her not.

Life

Juggling the heart and mind for eternity
Been called foolish bard, to a man witty
Yes, they change, and yet, stay the same
The lives in a life, have been called many names.

The teacher who teaches triumph in a fiasco
The word, significant to us, but nothing to the buried
low
The only thing, both blessed and cursed the most
That one syllable reverberated at every toast.

It's beauty is its whim, and it's love in the hardships
A celebration from the first glance, and glory on my
fingertips
Where uncertainty, is the thing most sure
Basking in the sun, under the blanket of azure.

Sometimes it's black, sometimes it's white
But all is harlequin under the light
Every fiction is real here, in different spheres
For "he who has eyes to see, and ears to hear".

Some say it's entwined, these two
Some are distinct in their 'me' and 'you'
But I say, you're in me and I'm in you

Shared is our love and shared is our rue.

Our journeys mark their starts together
And together we will go on forever
I may be gone, but my words will thrive
When I'll call out, that this is life.

My Friend / End

Love, where have you been?
Went away to commit another sin?
Left me to sit alone on the throne
My blackbird, away have you flown?

The night ascends, you should come too
Be this the night you will never rue
Splatters of blood are still on my cloak
But my darling, in blood you still soak.

Your accomplice, the love of your life
Dreams of today, nightmares of the afterlife
My King, I demand and you command
Then why tonight I bear your reprimand?

Two dark souls make one darker
When a win, it's you; a fiasco, and it's her
If it's not treachery, I don't know what is
You are a poison, devouring on me with every kiss.

My curse concealed in your vaunt
And to haunt is what I want
To love him was my whim
He was my sunshine when everything was grim.

But now he is here, and now will never see
tomorrow
Should I make the kill or forget all my sorrow?
Love, tell me now, where have you been?
I have lost again in your win.

I see blood, fresh out of me
Your dagger in my flesh, your face full of glee
I fall in the red sea, seeing you ascend
My own demon, the creation of a friend.

You walk to the throne, I am losing my sight
All shall end in this eternal night
But you slip in your red folly, and smash your head
And next I should know, we both are dead.

Black Heart

I killed the man who shot my dog
I strangled the angel who gave away the dialogue
I let them down on the streets of white
I shot them down in Devil's sight.

They cried for mercy, they cried of fear
But all I heard was cheer and cheer
I called them guilty for all their lies
Held them hostage and sued paradise

They said I had the Devil's mouth
I taught them hate and held the crowd
Deviated many from their tracks
'Cause I had the heart of black

They called me heartless in that hollow shade
When I denied giving to rodomontade
Took my mate and made him bait
And still expect me not to hate

I crushed their eyes
The way they crushed my soul
Instead of those diamonds
I hung around their necks burning coal

They said I had the Devil's sight
The fake happiness just didn't feel right
Blamed on others what I lack
'Cause I had the heart of black

They called me belladonna for the dark in me
And blamed it on my family
While my mongrel laid covered in pall
And for that I blame you all

They said I had the Devil's hand
Whatever I did was cursed and banned
Touched a house and made it a shack
'Cause I had the heart of black

Yes, my heart is black like night
And stars stick in me too
Black isn't dark, stars aren't all bright
But what you are for me, I am for you

Go and ponder what deed you did
Don't be back to do my bid
If I leave you alive, consider yourself dead
You didn't believe me before, why believe what I
just said?

The Bird Song

Peeping through my window I saw a bird
The eyes spoke it all, beak unuttered a word
It looked oddly familiar, like an old soul
Tapping for some water to be poured in the bowl

The bowl was full, it craved something else
Gazing back at it I felt helpless
"Sweet bird, do you want something to eat?"
The bird pecked at the ground, staring at my feet

It was her baby…lying on the floor
Chirping vaguely, looking so sore
 I knelt to pick it up, when I looked back at her
There was a "yes" in her eyes, but "no" in her whisper

If I touch the baby, she won't have it
My touch was a curse, and I was the git
But I can't let him die; I want him to flap his wings
I want him to nestle in the morning, and at night to sing

I picked up the baby, mouthed to the bird
"I will take care of him", and it looked like she heard

She blinked her eyes twice, signaling a "yes"
And left her baby, for me to caress

I looked outside, my face behind the bars
Then I looked at the baby, chirping in my arms
The prison door was black, black as my soul
Yet there was sunshine, peeping through a hole

And I thought to myself, this must be my salvation
For the people I slaughtered without hesitation
I took many lives, but today I saved one
If only I knew it back then, the deed would never be done.

NEON

Nighttime Thoughts

Sing me a song before I go
Tell me it's alright
Succumb to the fate with furore
It's just a matter of this night

Bide your time, complete your rhyme
Look forward to the adventures ahead
Every moment here has been sublime
Have a fiesta for the dead

This is not the end, you must comprehend
I am driving through the night
If possible, then to me just send
A little of your light

I drive ahead into the void
Passing through fellow cars
A constant speed to avoid
To be put up behind the bars

Yet I drive, I drive for hours
How many? I've lost the count
No time to rest under the bowers
Up, up I go, up on the mount

The pinnacle is overwhelming
Feels like a roller coaster
I'll shot out with the speed of light
Like a gun out from a holster

But wait, I am not going down
I am flying straight ahead
Flying, but why do I still feel the ground?
Oh wait, I'm still lying in my bed.

Queen of Swords

God created woman
And she became a queen
Her words and her sword
The reason for their spleen

She wore a crown
To cover her frown
No place to trust
But she was just

She wore no jewel
She was not cruel
She may be naïve
But she was not a fool

She saw it beyond
Dived into the void
Snapped all her bonds
With the paranoid

She would sit on her throne
Stained with blood
But that's what women are
Every month, every month

She never cried for help

She had herself, she was her own solace
She never stooped down, it's better to drown
Never compromised her grace

One day she faded into thin air
Some say it was the river
I will never believe a word they say
As long as she stares back at me from the mirror.

Time

Time, my time
If you could be bought with a dime
I could feel your highs and your lows
See my foes be friends and my friends turn to foes

"No amount of money bought a second of time"
A vagabond be king, make a saint commit a crime
Underestimate you, a man's greatest folly
Until he drops hard in the melancholy

Wish me no luck, but you
Wish me time, for it is true
Take me up, and drop me down
For my Time, to be King, you need no crown.

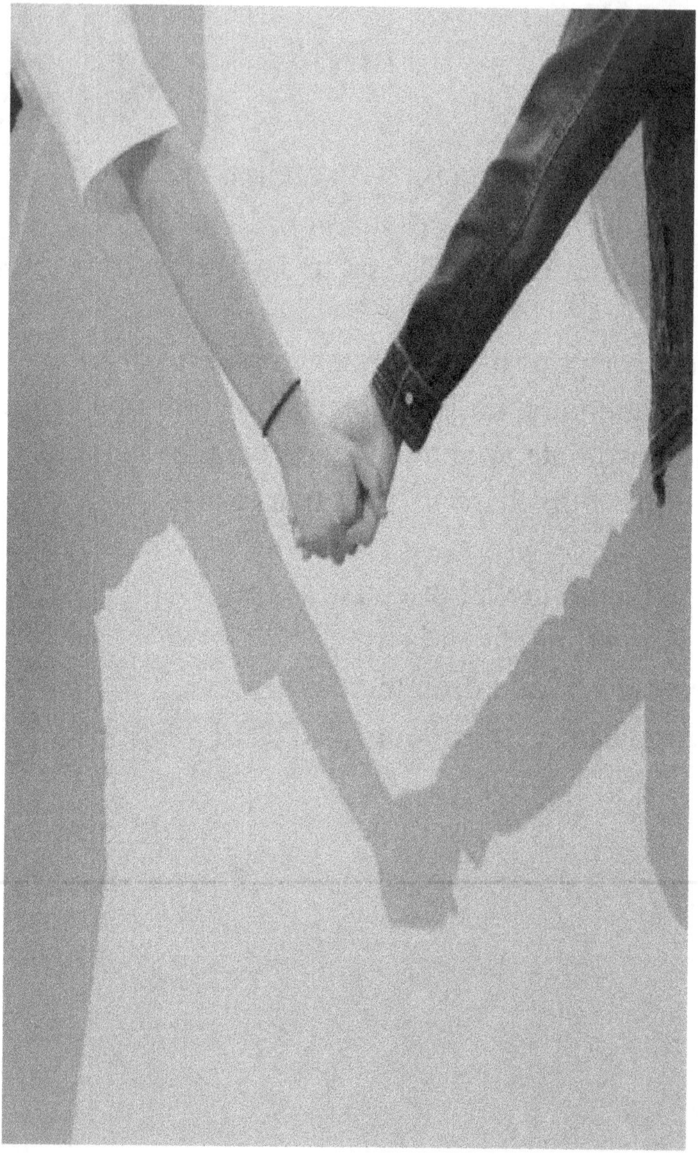

Friendship

Leaves rustling out the window, when the music
reached the crescendo
I sat down to write about my friend
From brainy to a bimbo, she'll leave you in a limbo
Through life, she transcends

Her name? I can't tell you that
Or you will want her too
We are like Viola and Cesario
Never wait till twelfth night for much ado

Friendship is the real Titanic
"All hail the unsinkable one!"
What candle it'll be, with a hatless wick
Futile till you make it burn

What else can bring euphoria?
Our hearts touching, our hands apart
No place as be as my utopia
Where every "Goodbye" marks a new start

Her and I, got one rule to comply
"A mate is no bait"
To be with others, you leave behind
The one you met by fate

The music has stopped, still someone's humming
A silhouette, blithe and latent
I turn around to see what's coming
The curtain conceals my friend

She asks me, "What are you writing about?"
"Friendship", is my reply
"Ours?" she asks with no trace of doubt
I nod and she asks why

"We are like bees in a honeycomb
Keeping it up together
And I promise my friend, till the day of our doom
It will stay forever"

A friend is me, and you and he
And she and we and all world is a friend
A loop profound, for the Earth is round
How can you expect it to end?

2020

2020

Who are we?
What have we done?
Spiraling in a skeptical reality
All bemused by the pun

Those kids walked down to school
Eyes holding dreams, face with a frown
Prepared already for the next day
To find their alma-maters shut down

Those tireless people praying for good
"All work and no leisure has left us sore"
Their prayers answered, festered in the
neighbourhood
And they couldn't go out no more

"All work and no play makes Jack a dull boy"
How well the situation overturned
Now "all play and no work has made Jack cloy"
"Where will the money come from?" his only
concern

The eerie silence fogs the windows
The inanimate streets feel dead
The honks and the gongs still blow

All inside our heads

Yet, there is serenity
Those chirruping proclaim the sunrise
So long since Mother looked that pretty
Wearing her green Crown of Paradise

Here in solitude, we self-reflect
Who are we? What have we done?
We've laughed so long when our Mother wept
It is time to work as one

People now work from home
The children study still
The world resides in their phones
And the phone on the window sill

Each day is now a festivity
Families getting along after eons
For a world in hues of black and white
We are the harlequin crayons

The time, like never seen before
Has now shown us many things
But will it still be like this forevermore
Or solely until this song you sing?

Theatre of Life

Tragedy puts out a gregarious approach
Of human kin and their sin
On the world's stage you're a performing roach
Your grief is someone else's grin

Act, with tact, it should leave an impact
Upon the reptile skin
The drama is no place for facts
The crocs have got no chin

The sickening rouge on the cheeks
Of man and of woman
One's plump with warmth while the other is bleak
Under the lifeless sun

That, is the play
You play every day
The King of morn, the Clown of night
In hours, you turn the shade of grey

Comedy cries wearing a crown
It applauds with appalled faces
It laughs on every time you frown
For putting you in those places

Your act is now of a Fool

Perform it with graveness
Be cautious in your insouciance
Think ways to be brainless

The leaders, the preachers, akimbo
Exclaim they see light ahead
Can you? "No!" we cry in limbo
"No wonder why you're worse than dead"

This is the comedy of tragedy
'They' cannot see it too
They'll say you got no eyes but beads
And will blame it on you

Sign a pact, with the stage
Tragic paint upon comical face
You're made of two, you'll die of one
So laugh with the stage, or sink in the Pun.

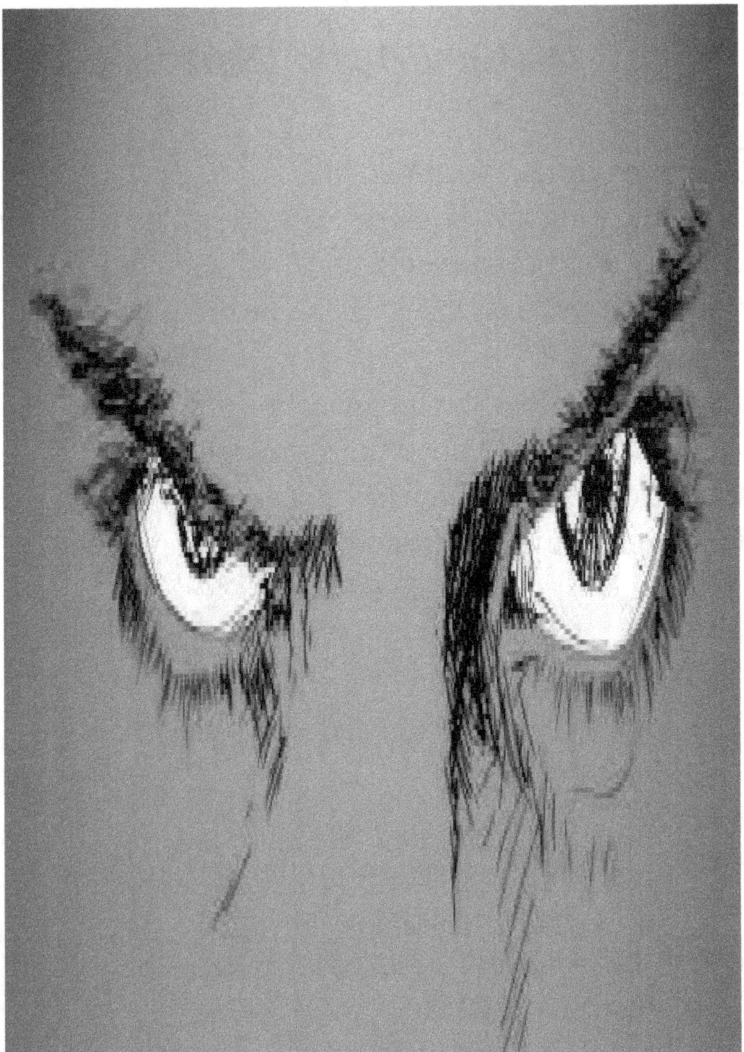

Rage on the Race

A quintessential specimen
Loving, caring and benign
Did you just fool yourself?
Pretending to be a closet when you are a shelf

Help, I just unleashed the macabre
The dark knight escaped the shiny armour
A sinner, a winner, they have been many things
Been high in their eyes, and dived through their
wings

Rage in the cage, an act of the sage
Your own fool and mage, differing in every page

Frail and fumbling, your soul
Vanity victorious, never accepting your role

A walking disaster
Faithful to no master
Faster! They are coming for you
The black cannot be hidden under the glittering hue

Seeking shelter in that one corner of mind
Where the real you can always unwind

Concealing yourself like a spider
But you failed at that too
Fascinated by your own web, spreading wider
Strangled upside down, without any clue

A mortal fiend
In every place intervened
Blamed curiosity for your guilty pleasures
Swallowed all at once the cursed treasure

Gibberish talk, like a stuck clock
Your lies are harder than a rock
Acts sleek, your body bleak
No sense what all you wreak

Candour, your biggest take
Floating in a bottomless lake
No song, no ballad, no rhyme can shake
Your roots, when your whole life has been a fake

 Dabbled in beliefs, never sensed relief
In that mind so fragile
For a living with emotions weak, no worse than a
freak
Turns out to be the most vile

All this while I've been talking to you
Yes you, the well-wisher of Hyde

Your attempts to turn turmoil into a queue
Made Jekyll to leave your side

I pity those apathetic brutes
But to warn them is like talking to lifeless roots
For when your sins take the form of your stoop
Comes the end of that endless loop

A fighter, a writer, you were everything
You still can be, if you promise your King
To learn the difference between a glass and a mirror
One can be fogged, painted and blocked, but you
can never bottle up a reflecting river.

The Wizard

Long ago when time was sand
All across the maiden land
Blew a severe blizzard
From that emerged a tiny wizard

A youth of the liveliest kind
With a cloak who appeared to have its own mind
A staff, no longer than a twig
Long hair that looked more like a wig

"Who art thee?" asked the Ancient Superior
Squeaked the wizard something, unable to hear
The Ancient barked, "Louder! You petty thing"
On this remark, the wizard started to sing

"I'm the one in which you all reside,
Thunder, experience, from mountains to pride,
I cannot be sought, fought, caught or bought,
As for my name Sir, I am Thought.

My cloak is experience and my staff is emotion
I am novel with every differing notion
My voice is a murmur now, but in a mind it booms
But beware of me; I can be somebody's success or
somebody's doom.

And you the Superior One, must be the Wall
A barrier in my way, all rigid and tall
But your arrogance is buoyant like a ball
What goes higher, eventually falls."

"You, Thought the Wizard, have no chance against
me
Go where you belong when you have the chance to
flee
No rain, no pain, no wind, no heat
Can infringe my power for I am concrete"

With this the Ancient Superior let out a roar
Utmost intentions to leave the wizard sore
Flung forward to demolish every single hair
But, to his surprise, was caught in mid-air

Experience the Cloak stood guard as a shield
Grew larger and larger and started to breathe
Emotion the Staff broke every brick
And all this happened in a single tick

Thought got promoted, and became Decision
With focused hands and a clear vision
With plenty arguments and interactions
Took his final form of Action

"Finally, my task is complete

It is time for my cycle to repeat
For head in the clouds when the ground holds feet
Is the greatest power that remains concrete."

Darkness

Born in a flash, dead with a flash
Gallivanting in the shadow lanes
Nightmare of the animated, solitude of a corpse
Eternal is your reign

Concealing whispers in your silence
Getting louder every night
No eyes, yet vigilance felt upon me
Hidden from the sight

I loathe you, because you are a coward
In light you take a flight
You hide behind me and take my form
The one behind every foul fight

You are cold, eerie, selfish, spineless, and shapeless
You dwell in every void
Inside me, inside them
Inside the earth freshly soiled

Here I am again, in your ambience
Your whispers are my thoughts
Your ghosts are now my entourage
I've become what I once fought

Dark but lucid, Satan's cupid
End of every hue
Immortal in this transient world
Everything begins from you

Impalpable, yet enticing
Those caught in your trap are all doomed
The vicious demons I once buried deep
Are now all exhumed

I think and see in your presence
There's no role of the eyes
You give the reason to imagine utopia
The last thing I'll see is you, before I see Paradise

How queer for us to bond in the night
We have become each other's part
You possess my soul, you possess my mind
But the light still got my heart

Cold can never be warm, damp can never be dry
The disparities can never be removed, even if we try
If all chose to be eternal, to death no one would
surrender
No grief would find the beauty in loss, no one would
be remembered

I love you, because you are eccentric

You soothe or give a fright
Behind me, you always have my back
Without you, there is no light

Here I am again, in your ambience
All you ever whispered were my thoughts
You reflect the psyche, the real visage
I've learned the truth that was once mistaught.

The Moon and the Sea

I need you and you need me
We are like the moon and the sea
The moon, unknown of her beauty
Shyly glances at the sea
The sea, a vast expanse of crystal purity
Is her mirror
She looks down at her reflection
Nothing but mere perfection
How bias is the sea!
He reflects the best in her
The blemishes concealed
She is content with the sea
The sea, the mirror of her life
Realistic in his approach, yet persuadable
Shows his love for the moon through this fable:
We are like the moon and the sea
I need you, and you need me.

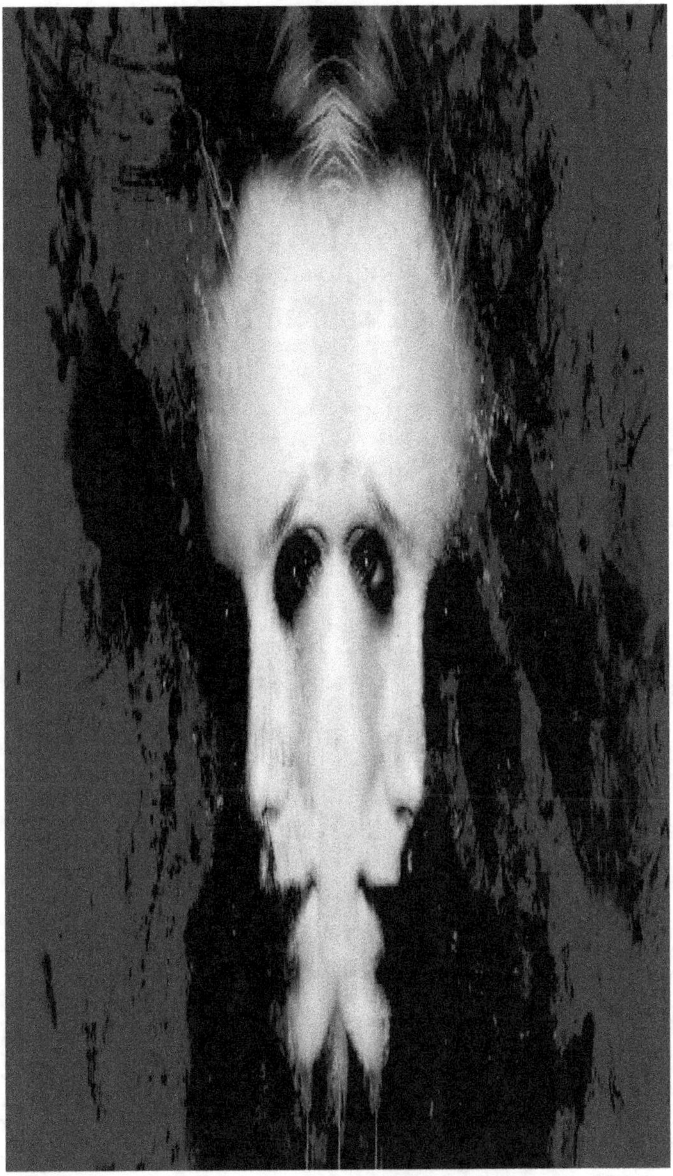

Psychopath

My blood is cold but my hands are warm
By brushing them against the grass of the lawn
The blades wound my hand and blood trickles down
Yet sometimes I laugh, sometimes I frown

The candour in my smile
Conceals my intentions vile
My eyes gleam bright in the light
But they are dead deep inside

My melodious voice hides the serpent's snare
I tell them I'm their friend, but no one dares
My glossy hair may look smooth; the roots are
nothing but rough
Those fools ignore my lack of mercy, and praise that
I am tough

My conversation is nothing but treachery
As part of my plan
I'll still lure, gallivant, and be carefree
Even if I killed a man

I can't remember when I felt love
But this is not my fault
They never sent it with me from above

And hid my heart in a vault

My psyche is extremely conflicting
It does not know how to choose
Will it be called an evil thing,
If I torture one or two?

You don't understand, you don't know me
I have truth in my lies
When I say I feel nothing
Neither your sorrow nor your cries

I don't have time for mourning
I'm bound by invisible ropes
I can't expiate myself, if this helps
When I'm already a corpse

My insanity comes from my weakness
My strength takes me to the hellish path
My people never helped me with my freakiness
Yet I am the Psychopath.

Ms. Imaginary

She walks around me like a doe
She soothes me deep and takes all my woe
Her words are like a lullaby
The child inside my starts to cry

I feel her but I can't see
Is she real or a fantasy?
The thought of it hurts like a wound
Like a wolf, I cry at the moon

My Ms. Imaginary
Why should you leave in such a hurry?
I try to conceal, but it won't heal
I know I have to bury you down, in my memory

Her close distance mocks me down to grave
The hope to last makes me remain brave
Her brittle heart seems to mould mine
But infinity is never found in line

I cry but no one hears me
Is she a savior or the death of me?
The thought of it makes me feel soon
In a fake world I'll be a real loon

My Ms. Imaginary
Why you should leave in such a hurry?
I try to conceal, but it won't heal
I know I have to bury you down, in my memory

My disappearance is your presence
You are my purpose, my life's true essence
Sometimes I see you in me
Wondering if I'm real or Ms. Imaginary?

Who am I?

When I cry, tears fall from the sky
The wind wipes them off
I ask myself, "Who am I?"
To receive a touch so soft

The mountains are my reputation
They stand upright and high
The pinnacle is my salvation
I wonder, who am I?

My blood flows like the brimming river
I conceal the tot so shy
The liquor of joy is what I savour
I wonder, who am I?

The tranquil mind is the mysterious woods
There reside the truthful lies
The battle of saints and raging crooks
I wonder, who am I?

The air fades like a puff of smoke
How precious are my sighs!
My entrails go feeble, my hope broke
I wonder, who am I?

The corpse decays like memory
The benign soul is about to fly
The bird is finally at liberty
I wonder, who am I?

The visage turns into a mirror for all
They seek what they desire
The reflection is blocked by concrete walls
I wonder, who am I?

My life will turn into a mere fable
As time passes by
The words would be defamed to labels
Still wondering who am I?

My identity is still unknown to me
Am I it's part or is it a part of me?
But what I know is that I live beyond this life
My 'real home' is where I'll thrive.

CURSURI
CONTABILITATE
(Dări de seamă)
CU Programare
CONTABILI
CURSURI
CONTABIL

Words

The stories close to the heart never fade away
The lexemes and soliloquies makes the mind sway
The unfathomable lines look at the shallow mind
with pity
How can it find solace in false alacrity?

The words knock at the door of the empty brain
"Let us in!" they cried with sorrow and pain
"We have the power to provide you tranquility,
Our signature is our fidelity,

We'll be your mentors, our shine on your visage,
Fill yourself with emotions, not gaspillage,
We can heal your heart; we can give you wounds,
But we are worthless to imbeciles and loons."

The brain finally opened the door
And let the words flow deep in the core
Till that day they have not left my brain
Now I'm a poet who's called insane

People are unable to comprehend what I mean
They cannot imagine what I have already seen
I follow my words like a sheep's herd
And they take me to another world

I find solitude with these words of mine
They make me imagine above the line
Even when I'm gone, they'll stay after me
Fulfilling their promise of fidelity

The stories and fables are nothing but words
They are meant to be said, they are meant to be heard
My life is words, my words are alive
The abstract in them conceals the meaning of life.

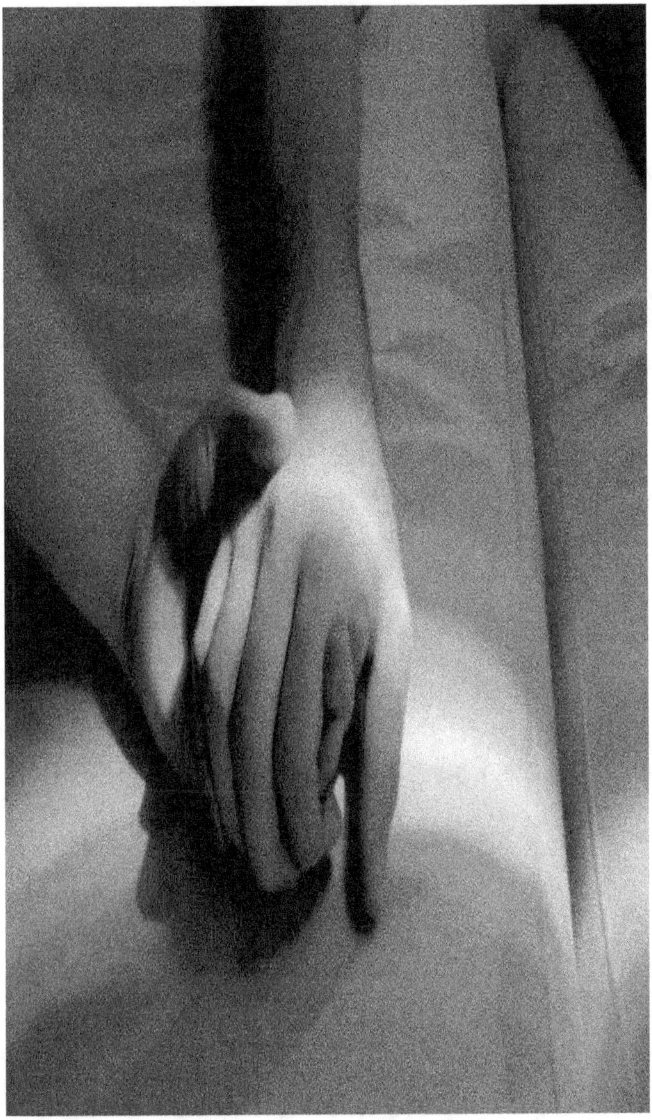

Adieu

"Life is simple, make a new start"
My mind is ready; it's a no from the heart
I am complete, and now I see the heavenly view
With this my friend, I bid you adieu

The sparkling lights don't woo me anymore
The fame and flattery has left me sore
I see myself standing in the Purgatory queue
With this my friend, I bid you adieu

The love and care gave me strength
The spiritual bond of immeasurable length
But now I want to feel something new
With this my friend, I bid you adieu

My journey may begin again very soon
Until then people think of me as a loon
I am something, understood by a few
With this my friend, I bid you adieu

Don't shed your tears, I have conquered death
I am not limited by mere breaths
I will always be yours, I will live for you
With this my friend, I bid you adieu.

Nature

I gaze upon the stars of every sort
Stuck in the whirlpool of my thoughts
Awestruck watching a leaf grow
How a rabbit hides in its burrow

Nature is the soul of the world
Boundless to the description of words
How uniquely every tree is queued
Artistically, like a woman's pulchritude

The fragrance of flowers is the only thing I smell
The dawn and dusk has captivated me under its spell
The creatures with abilities to fly and swim
A wolf's howl, a hyena's grin

 In the woods, I hear the cacophony
Of sour lemons and sweet honey
How lucky! Nature has no greed for money
But only longs for peace and harmony

Alas! My nature is crying for mercy
To the destruction humanity is blind to see
The beauty has turned into dust in flashes
What are left are just carcasses and ashes

The kingdom of nature lies in shatters
The foolish human says, "Doesn't matter!"
But what will happen when air turns to soot
Will you eat money as your food?

Save the nature, you still have time
Become immortal through this powerful rhyme
The animals' laughs are so precious to hear
Make the waters sweet again and clear

And the nature will sing again its song
Faded with time and forgotten so long
Of grizzly bears and dogs' tails
Of how fishes are set to sail

Comprehended only by a few
Nature is the heavenly view
That gives hope of something new
Made, with love, only for you.

Hope

I took my flight in brazen wind
With latent clues and a few hints
Ceased at the heaven's delight
The Creator was present in my sight

The grace that ended every feud
The hands that created a woman's pulchritude
The mind chiseled with great depth
The name inhaled through every breath

I searched for words, didn't know what to say
To the hermit who lit my way
Forgive me My Lord! For I have sinned
Surprisingly, he relaxed and grinned

"My child, what happened was meant to be
For humanity never had the power to see
The destruction could not have lasted forever
The best I have will always be savoured"

But Lord how can I apologize?
For the foolishness and decisions made, unwise
What more do I have to lose
This is not the life that I would choose

"My dear, you're innocent and naïve to the world
The reason why your prayer was heard
Have faith, for humanity cannot die
As long as in you, I am alive."

S.C.I.E.N.C.E.

I climb the stars in the night
I walk the sun on the bridge of light
On reaching the top, I call hello!
With a halt, my voice echoes

Night is silver
The day is gold
Blue is the river
The diamond I hold

For whatever reason I'm writing this poem
Is not for my imaginary heights
It's just I'm just bored, from xylem and phloem
I just want to escape SCIENCE!!!

Inside Out

Little do we know of ourselves,
But more of this world
Sometimes I should ask myself
Was it true what I heard?

The solitary mind prays for friends
The desperate call for love never ends
The melancholic soul continues to sing
For salvation that the faith will bring

My miserable life cries to know
But what I hear is the worldly woe
How someone cheated on his beloved lover
How everyone is under the faux pleasant cover

What are we doing? What have we done?
No one is saved from it but equal to none
But I'll grow strong and rescue myself out
To change and help the blinded crowd

I know it's hard to shut the doors
The lovely choir turns to deadly growls
But if we follow the true commands
We'll reach the aim that He demands

Believe, when it's dark like inferno
Hear, even if the speaker is your foe
Talk, even where there's no one to hear
Love, without any bounds and fear.

Lament of a Fangirl

I look at the blank time that I bought
It's been long but my feelings are still caught
Wondering what will happen if I
Meet the one whom I admire?

My life is clutched in fantasies
Everyday thinking, "Marry me please!"
For him, I'll leap the continents and swim the seven seas
But alas! He doesn't know me

To spell perfection I spell out his name
I look beyond his riches and fame
If only I had a chance with thee
Alas! He doesn't know me

I blame him for my expectations high
To say I'm over him would be a lie
Your birthday is my festivity
Alas! If only you knew me

Whenever I see you, I fall for you more
It's something I've never felt before
The people around you are so lucky
I wish if only one of them was me

When you talk, it feels like you're talking to me
You don't even know, but you're already a part of
my family
I laugh when your face is full of glee
Wish those moments you shared, were shared with
me

I know in my mind I am not right
You are the reason I can't sleep at night
Wondering if I would sleep soundly
In my bed, if you were beside me

Praying every moment to time for a miracle
That we would meet, and sparks would fly fickle
I would finally touch you, and feel that you're real
I would present you my love in an envelope with a
seal

And that would consist a letter for you
Singing how much I love you
For I know all good things take time
But I know one day, you will be mine.

Flairs and Glairs, a platform by a student for the students. We are esteemed youth struggling to carve out our path for our future and we follow a basic mindset Since everyone is not born with all-round skills. Joining hands with people who are born to execute it with perfection is the best way to evolve. Self-Evolution is the need of the hour but, evolving as a community is what we strive for. The initiative as kickstarted by, Founder- Mr. Shubham Shah with the motive to utilize the skillset and talent of writing has now a team of 10+ people who are actively participating into newer forms of learning and discovering talents among youngsters. We Provide platform and services like Publishing opportunities, Open mics, Workshops, Hands-on training. Operating with Brand Name of Flairs and Glairs (Publication House), we offer the chance of elevating a passionate writer to an esteemed author With Brand name Teekhe Zasbaaat. We bring to you an opportunity to get accustomed with the Public Speaking and Presenting of Thoughts along with regular challenges to brush up your inking spirit. The newest initiative to extend our services we introduced in a new writing Platform- The Glittering Fables and Ink Over Tears.

We Choose to Fly Like A Falcon than to be a Leg Pulling Crab.

To Know More: Infoline – 7781900870

Mail Us At-

flairsandglairs@gmail.com / info@flairsandglairs.in

Or Visit is at

www.flairsandglairs.com / www.flairsandglairs.in

Social Handles- @flairsandglairs @teekhezasbaaat